My Little Everest

CANADIAN CATALOGUING IN PUBLICATION DATA

Culver, Dan, 1952-1993
My Little Everest

ISBN 1-55039-105-4

I. Title.
PS8555.U4835M9 2000 jC813'.54 C00-910179-9
PZ7.C907My 2000

Sono Nis Press gratefully acknowledges the support of the Canada Council for the Arts and the Province of British Columbia, through the British Columbia Arts Council.

Cover and book design by Jim Brennan.
Photos by Dan Culver.

Published by
Sono Nis Press
PO Box 5550, Stn. B
Victoria, BC V8R 6S4
tel: (250) 598-7807
sono.nis@islandnet.com
http://www.islandnet.com/sononis/

Distributed in the U.S. by
Orca Book Publishers
Box 468
Custer, WA 98240-0468
1-800-210-5277

Partial proceeds from the sale of this book go to The Dan Culver Follow Your Dream Foundation.
Printed and bound in Canada by Friesen's Printing.

my little Everest

a story about dealing with fear

Dan Culver

Victoria B.C. Canada

Foreword

Dan Culver and I have something very important in common: a belief that big dreams can come true.

While Dan's dream was to climb and conquer the world's highest mountain, Mount Everest, and raise awareness for the environment, mine was to wheel around the world to raise awareness of the potential of people with disabilities.

Dan and I made our dreams come true by believing in ourselves, overcoming our fears, and encouraging strong teamwork. In this inspiring story of Martyn and his nephew Ryan, Dan shows that no matter what you've accomplished or how many peaks you've climbed, it's natural to get frightened when a seemingly impossible challenge comes your way. I'm sure Dan must have looked up in awe at the peak of Everest and wondered how he'd ever reach it. I too, became scared while on my Man in Motion World Tour, wondering if I would ever finish the journey.

"My little Everest" is a name that young Ryan gives to each of his fears, from paddling against harsh waves and wind, to pursuing a dream of playing on his school's soccer team. Though some of us may never set foot on a high mountain peak, we all have our own little Everests to climb. My Everest was conquered when I finally came home after more than two years of wheeling around the world.

Whatever your little Everest is, remember that no mountain is too high to climb, and no dream too big to achieve. Follow young Ryan's example: believe that anything is possible.

Rick Hansen
President and CEO
Rick Hansen Institute

Preface

I met Dan Culver after his 1990 Mount Everest climb, and was married to him for nine months before he summited K2, the world's second-highest mountain, and fell to his death on his descent in July 1993. One would think that a man of Dan's risk-taking and adventurous feats would be free of fear, but he was not. He had found a way to accept and conquer his fears and insecurities, so that he was not limited by them as he took action towards fulfilling his dreams. From the time he was a young boy, Dan had many dreams and goals for himself, and he believed that people were happiest when they listened to their inner ambitions and worked towards them.

As Dan and I joined in marriage in 1992, he welcomed my twelve-year-old son, Ryan, into his heart and loved teaching him all sorts of things about life. Dan observed Ryan's eagerness to learn and took great pleasure in guiding and encouraging Ryan to use his imagination, to create his dreams and goals, and to find the courage to make them come to life. Dan told Ryan that courage was not fearlessness, but rather feeling his fear and not letting it stop him.

My Little Everest is a story that Dan created from his lifelong experiences, his Everest expedition, and his friendship with Ryan, in order to share his knowledge about fear with others of all ages. His hope was that young people and their parents or grandparents or aunts or uncles or friends would read it and talk about their own stories of living their dreams and overcoming their fears.

May you enjoy Dan's spirit expressed in his words and let them inspire you to stretch beyond your own limitations to realize your dreams.

Patricia Culver

It was a glorious day, a golden Sunday in September, the sort of day that makes you glad to be alive. The crisp scent of autumn was softened by the warmth of late summer, and there were only patches of snow on the mountains around North Vancouver. Eleven-year-old Ryan Connor perched on the edge of the dock, his favourite place to go whenever he needed to think about things. Often, he liked to come here to put his crab trap down to see if he could catch anything; from the dock, he could watch the boats go by, and wonder about the people on them.

This morning, though, Ryan was feeling too unhappy to pay much attention. So, it wasn't until he pulled up his trap that he noticed his Uncle Martyn approaching by canoe. Martyn lived on the other side of Indian Arm, the ocean inlet where Ryan and his parents lived. There were no roads to Martyn's cabin; whenever he wanted to go anywhere, he went by boat.

Martyn was Ryan's favourite uncle. A climber and an adventurer, he often travelled to exciting, distant places; in fact, he had just returned from the top of Mount Everest! Yet, whenever he was home, he always made time for his nephew. Martyn rarely gave advice, but he had an interesting way of looking at things.

"Hey, Ryan!" Martyn called as he steered towards the dock, his red-blond hair bright in the morning sunlight.

"Morning, Uncle Martyn." Ryan steadied the canoe as it came alongside, grabbing the painter and tying it up to the ring on the dock.

"Thanks, pal. Great day, eh?"

Ryan's blue eyes dimmed. "It's okay."

"Why the long face?"

Ryan shrugged. "Nothing, I guess." He watched as Martyn stowed away his paddle and life jacket, and then focused on his reflection in the water. "I'm thinking about skipping school tomorrow."

Martyn sat down beside his nephew, and for a while, there was only the sound of the water lapping against the dock.

"Last time we talked, you said that you liked your new school."

"It's all right."

"So what's the problem?"

"They're picking the school's tournament soccer team tomorrow."

"And?"

"They only pick fifteen kids." Ryan stared past his reflection. "You have to be really good."

"Are you good?"

Ryan's gaze shifted briefly toward his uncle, and then returned to the water. "I don't know."

"Don't you want to find out?"

"I'm not sure. In my old school, my coach thought that I was pretty good, but the guys at this school–I've seen them practising. Some of them are awesome, and they've all played together before, and . . ." Ryan's voice trailed off.

"And you're afraid?"

Ryan's face clouded. "Yeah, I guess so."

Martyn regarded his nephew thoughtfully. "Do you think that skipping school will make that fear disappear?"

Puzzled, Ryan looked up at his uncle. "Maybe."

"Ryan, fear doesn't go away just because you hide from something that frightens you. You carry it with you until the next time. And every time you run away, it tightens its control over you. The truth is, Ryan, most of us are afraid sometimes, but we still need to do what we feel is important. Otherwise, we let our fears become our masters."

Ryan looked at his uncle, and then turned away. "I guess so. But it still feels easier just to skip out."

Martyn smiled, then nodded in the direction of his cabin across the inlet. "Hey, I dropped by to see if you wanted to visit. It seems like a long time since you've been over."

"Oh yeah, that'd be great!" Ryan's face brightened.

"Okay, why don't you run up and tell your folks that you're coming with me."

"Right!"

Ryan took off up the path to the house. Martyn watched him until Ryan's curly brown hair bobbed out of sight; then he turned his attention to the inlet. It was a perfect day for a paddle. There was little wind, and the sun was warm. Martyn could see small whitecaps midway; as usual, there was some chop there, but only a light wind, and the rest of the inlet looked calm. Martyn climbed in the canoe, put on his life jacket, and readied the paddles.

A few minutes later, Ryan joined his uncle, careful to step into the centre of the canoe to avoid banging it against the dock. He knew how fond his uncle was of his canoe; he had lovingly restored it from a worn and faded boat to its present, gleaming condition. All the dings and nicks had been patiently filled and sanded, and the whole canoe stained and polished until you could almost see yourself in the reflection.

As they pushed away from the dock, Ryan finished tying his life jacket and picked up his paddle. "Which side should I paddle on, Uncle Martyn?"

"You paddle on the left; I'll take the right."

After a few strokes, the two canoeists found their rhythm. Ryan relaxed into it, feeling the canoe slicing through the water. For a while, there was just the splash of their paddles, the gleam of the sun on the ocean, and the cry of the gulls. But, as they left the protection of the coast, they felt the wind begin to pick up strength. They could see patches of ripples forming on the water ahead; moments later, they felt waves rocking the canoe. Then, as they reached the midway point, they were struck by blasts of wind funnelling down from a slot between the mountains.

"Paddle hard!" Martyn yelled as he shifted his weight to keep the canoe from tipping. The wind almost whipped his words away before they reached Ryan in the bow. Ryan took a few more paddle strokes, and then fear gripped him as the canoe reacted violently to the wind and bucked wildly in the waves. He dropped his paddle into the canoe and clung to the sides of the boat.

"Ryan!" hollered Martyn. "Keep paddling! I know you're afraid, but don't let your fear take over!"

Ryan gritted his teeth, tears stinging his eyes. His uncle had never shouted at him before; worse, Ryan sensed a touch of fear along with the urgency in Martyn's voice. Trembling, Ryan grabbed his paddle and began to dig it hard into the rough water on his side of the canoe. At times, the bow was thrown so high by the waves that his paddle couldn't reach the water, but Ryan's hard paddling kept his fear at bay.

Finally, they struggled through the middle of the inlet. The gusts of wind became less forceful and the waves grew smaller. As they approached the dock in front of Martyn's house, the water was calm once more, and Ryan relaxed his tense grip on the paddle.

Martyn reached out to pull the canoe up to the dock. "Sorry for yelling at you out there, pal–but we'd have been in trouble if you'd stopped paddling." He climbed out of the canoe, and started to secure it to the landing.

"I'm sorry–I got scared when the wind hit us like that," Ryan muttered, slicking his wet hair away from his face.

Martyn watched his young nephew climb out of the canoe. "Don't apologize for being afraid, Ry. Everyone's afraid at some time. It's what you do when you're afraid that matters."

Ryan looked up at his uncle. "You're never afraid, though! You couldn't be afraid and do the things you do, like climbing Mount Everest!"

"Oh, you couldn't be more wrong, Ryan!" Martyn smiled. "I've been afraid many times in my life, including on Mount Everest. Just because you've dealt with lots of fear in your past doesn't mean that fear is behind you. You still have to face it, again and again, in all your new experiences."

Ryan was crestfallen. His own fear was still reverberating through him. He didn't want to hear that his heroic uncle had fears and weaknesses, just like everybody else, just like him. As Ryan watched, Martyn put the bumpers between the canoe and the dock, so that the canoe wouldn't get scratched. When he was done, he turned to his nephew, putting his arm around the boy's shoulders. "Fear's nothing to be ashamed of. C'mon. Bring your paddle and life jacket and let's go up to the house."

Martyn's cabin, like his canoe, had been restored with care. It had been a rundown shack, but now it was a comfortable, rustic home. Inside, the gleaming wood trim enclosed many shelves full of books, as well as fascinating souvenirs from Martyn's world travels.

Ryan loved to explore the cabin, looking at the artwork and souvenirs and asking Martyn for the stories behind them. Like the worn climbing stick that had belonged to Ryan's great-grandfather, who had also been a climber, or the tiny skull of a fox that Martyn had found on Baffin Island. And the books! Books about climbing, about sailing, and about explorers from the past, like Christopher Columbus. Ryan felt that he could spend days just exploring this one room, and still not see everything. Martyn had spent many years sailing; to Ryan, being in his uncle's tidy, organized cabin felt like being on a ship. Martyn's place was so different from Ryan's own home, or those of his friends. It was a special haven than Ryan found endlessly fascinating.

As they entered the cabin, Ryan noticed that the sturdy wooden table in the dining area was covered with photographs. "What are you doing with all those?"

"Oh, those are my photos from Everest. I've been trying to organize them to make a scrapbook about the expedition. I haven't gotten too far, though," he added sheepishly. "Every time I pick up a picture, I start daydreaming about the great experiences I had on the climb." Martyn moved to the stove, lit it, put on the kettle, and then took two cups and the makings for hot chocolate out of the cupboard.

"Can we look at the pictures?" Ryan pleaded. Often, Martyn needed lots of persuading to talk about his adventures, even though Ryan loved to hear about them.

This time, though, he agreed right away. "Sure, if you want. I'll just finish making this hot chocolate. I think we both need it after that wet ride!" He poured the water into the cups, stirred, and added a marshmallow to Ryan's, just the way he liked it. Then, setting the cups down on the table, he took a seat beside Ryan. "Where shall we start?"

"At the beginning, of course!" Ryan grinned, then sipped cautiously at his hot chocolate.

Martyn sorted through the photographs, pulling out a few to show his nephew. "Here's Kathmandu, the biggest city in Nepal. We had to fly there to begin the expedition. Then, we had to hike for two weeks just to get to the base of the mountain."

Martyn smiled at the memory. "It was so beautiful passing along the villages and countryside. It was a long walk, but along the way our team talked about the plans for the climb–and about our lives back home. We used the time to get to know each other better."

Ryan pulled some other colourful pictures towards him. "You've got lots of pictures here of people–are they from Nepal?" His uncle nodded, and Ryan studied the figures in the photographs. "They sure look different from us. What are they like?"

Again, Martyn smiled in recollection. "Those are the Sherpas, the people who live in the high country near the base of Everest. They are an amazing people–strong, resilient, and very friendly. They have a great sense of humour, and they loved it whenever we were silly or played practical jokes on each other."

Martyn took a sip of hot chocolate, then went on. "We met lots of Sherpa children on the hike to the base of Everest. They were very curious about us, and when we stopped to rest or make camp, they would come up to us, shyly. A lot of our equipment was strange to

monoflex

them." Martyn handed Ryan a photograph. "I let these two small children look at my camera and listen to my tape recorder. They were amazed that music came out of the earphones."

"They were probably just amazed at the weird music you listen to!" Ryan teased.

Martyn laughed. "Well. That just proves that there are generation gaps wherever you go!"

Turning back to the photos, he continued. "For part of the trek to the mountain we used yaks to carry our equipment. In Nepal, where

people have so little, animals like yaks that can work hard and make money for their owners are very valuable. The owners often decorate their yaks by putting bells around their necks and braiding ribbons into their tails. But we had to be careful on the steep trails that we didn't step in front of a yak–they've been known to use their horns to toss people off the trail!

"Finally, we arrived at our base camp at the foot of the mountain. We rested there for a few days with the Sherpa companions who would be going up the mountain with us. Before we began to climb, they chanted prayers for our safety and hung prayer flags on ropes at the corners of our camp. The Sherpas believe that the prayers written on these flags are blown by the wind into the heavens, and that they keep climbers safe. We were very willing to do anything that would make the climb safer, so we helped the Sherpas put up the flags."

Martyn paused. "I had another reason for hanging up those flags. By climbing Everest, I was hoping to call attention to two wilderness areas here in British Columbia, two beautiful valleys that really need to be protected from environmental damage. I wanted to dedicate my ascent of Everest to those valleys. So, I put up my banners, along with the Sherpa flags, for good luck." Martyn smiled at his nephew. "I wanted to take as much luck up with me as I could!"

For a few moments, Ryan stared at the picture of the colourful flags. Then, he turned to look at Martyn. "That climb must have been really dangerous."

"Sure, in places. One of the most dangerous parts was at the beginning, when we had to go through a very steep and treacherous section of glacier called the 'Khumbu Icefall.' In order to take supplies to our camps higher on the mountain, we needed to go up and down this section many times, carrying food, ropes, and other equipment on shaky ladders across the crevasses. A crevasse is a crack in the glacier caused when the ice shifts. There were lots on the mountain, and some of them can be over one hundred feet deep, so we were always very careful around them."

"Were they special ladders?" Ryan asked.

Martyn laughed. "Nope. Just good old standard aluminum ladders, like your dad uses to climb up to clean the eaves."

"And you had to go over them again and again?" Ryan's eyes widened.

"Yup. But in the end, it was good practice taking our gear up the

mountain. It really got us in shape for the tough climb we had to get to the top. Higher on the mountain we had to climb very steep slopes, and we had to use crampons to keep us from slipping."

Martyn noticed the puzzled look on Ryan's face and explained. "You remember before I left I showed you my climbing boots, and the special attachments with the spikes? Those are crampons, and you need them to get a good grip on ice or snow."

Ryan nodded. "Yeah, I remember–like really sharp golf shoes. Cool!"

Ryan studied the photograph. Then he looked up and met his uncle's gaze. "Weren't you afraid of falling?"

Martyn's face grew thoughtful. "Sure, I was afraid sometimes. But I couldn't let my fear stop me. Sometimes, I'd need to talk to myself. I'd say, 'Okay, Martyn, I know you're afraid, but you have to move on anyway. If you stay here, you'll be unhappy and afraid, and you won't ever know what it feels like on the top of this mountain.'"

His voice softened as he went on. "You know, the hardest thing for me on Everest was silencing the little voice inside me that tried to tell

me all the reasons I wouldn't get to the top. When I looked at our team of climbers I saw people much more experienced and skilled than I am. It would have been easy to believe that they might get to the summit without me. I needed to believe in myself–I've seen again and again how important it is to have a strong belief in yourself. If you're able to see yourself succeeding, then it's almost as if you change your luck so that things work out the way you want."

"Does that really work–just thinking you're going to succeed?"

"Sure. That's how my climbing partner, Alex, and I planned our attempt at the summit. The weather had been really bad for days. Other climbers were convinced that the storms were going to continue and that there was no chance of getting to the top. But Alex and I thought positively, and we climbed to our high camp at the South Col at 26,100 feet, trusting that the weather would improve. Even though the wind was howling outside, we stayed there in our little mountaineering tents for two nights, which was longer than most people thought safe to stay at that altitude.

“Fortunately for us, on the morning of our third day at the South Col, the wind died down. We knew that this was probably our only chance to go to the summit, since we were getting weaker every day that we stayed at that high altitude. It was still a huge challenge to climb the final 3,000 feet to the top. The snow was soft and difficult to climb in. The thin air at that height made it very hard to breathe. Many times I wondered what made me push on. I thought about quitting. Lots. But something inside me just wouldn’t let me turn back.

"After an exhausting climb, we finally made it to the top of Mount Everest. We were excited, but we also knew that the dangers weren't over yet–we still had to get back down!"

For a moment, Martyn was quiet, and then he continued. "Of course, we took pictures–and tried to take in that amazing, unbelievable view. For that brief moment in time, we were standing higher than all the people in the world." Martyn's eyes grew distant, and then he turned to Ryan. "There we were, on top of the world. I felt humble, small, and very grateful to be there."

Martyn grew silent, and Ryan tried to imagine what his uncle must be feeling, what he must have felt on Everest, standing above the world. For a moment, Ryan almost forgot to breathe. "How would you have felt if you hadn't made it to the top?"

Martyn smiled. "I would have been disappointed–that's for sure!" Thoughtfully, he continued. "I still would have felt good about myself, though, for giving it my best effort. You know, sometimes, no matter how hard you try to reach your goals, the weather or some other thing outside your control can stop you from getting there."

Martyn picked up another photo and passed it to Ryan. "The scariest part of the climb for me was going back down the mountain from the summit. I was tired, and some of the sections were very steep. I remember being particularly afraid as I climbed down the Hillary Step."

"There was a step called Hillary?" Ryan looked at his uncle as if he'd lost a few too many brain cells up at the South Col.

Martyn laughed, shaking his head. "Not that kind of Hillary. Sir Edmund Hillary and Sherpa Tenzing Norgay were the first people to ever reach the summit of Everest way back in 1953–long before you were born, kiddo! The step is actually the route Hillary took across the crest of a ridge to get to the summit. It takes a lot of skill and concentration to follow that route, and Alex and I didn't have a climbing rope to protect us, so a fall from there would have meant falling thousands of feet. I told myself to be very careful as I climbed down this section. And I needed to remind myself that I could handle each challenge as it came along."

Thoughtfully, Ryan studied the photographs. Then he looked at his

Sunice

uncle. "I used to think that you never got scared. You're always doing such awesome stuff." Ryan glanced at the pictures in front of him. "But you'd have to be crazy not to be scared sometimes–you just didn't let it stop you from doing what you really wanted to do."

Martyn placed his hand lightly on Ryan's shoulder. "That's it, Ry. Facing your fears is one of the most important things you can learn to do. Too many people never figure out that lesson. They let their fears keep them from getting to where they want to go.

"It took me a long time to realize that we all have fears about something. The people who appear the bravest are just like you and me–they feel afraid sometimes too. What makes the people we admire stand out is that they don't let their fears stop them from doing what they believe in.

"When we climbed to the summit there were definitely moments of fear. If we hadn't pushed through that fear and kept on climbing, we would have missed out on the incredible feeling that we experienced being on top of the world, knowing that we'd reached our goal!"

Ryan looked up at his uncle. "That's why you yelled at me in the canoe, right? I was letting my fear stop me. I needed to push past it, like you did on Everest." Ryan paused, remembering. "You know, when I did start paddling again, even though the fear was still there, I felt better, sort of stronger."

"That's it, Ryan! That's what happens when you face your fear. You do get stronger inside." Martyn smiled. "But you still need to be ready to do it all over again. Like the next time that you face Everest, or choppy water . . . or soccer tryouts."

Ryan's face brightened. "Hey–you know what? I think I'm going to call anything that I'm afraid of 'my little Everest.' That way, I'll remember not to let my fears stop me–just like you didn't let your fears stop you on Everest."

Martyn nodded. "Sounds good. Everyone has different ways of dealing with their fears–you'll have to figure out what works for you. Some people might think of fear as a bird that they hold in their hands, and when they raise their arms, their fears fly away. Others need to face

sunice

their fears and take action in order to move through them. Each of us needs to learn the ways that work best for us."

"So what were some of the ways you used–what did you do on Everest?"

"What worked for me on Everest, and I've used it often through the years, is something called visualization: instead of thinking of all my problems, I show my mind pictures of things working out successfully. I do this over and over again, until my mind believes it. This often leads to things working out the way I want. I've heard that many athletes use these visualization techniques to improve their game."

Ryan considered this for a minute. "So instead of thinking about getting hurt, you thought about climbing to the top?"

"That's exactly right. On our Everest climb I would lie in my tent every night and picture myself climbing safely to the top. It took many nights of practice before I could safely climb the mountain in my mind. After that, I had the confidence I needed to make the actual climb, without my fear getting in the way."

"That's awesome!"

Martyn grinned. "Yeah, it is. And if you practise this kind of thinking, it can make lots of problems easier to deal with. And it doesn't just have to be about problems–you can visualize good things getting even better."

"Well, if it worked that well for you on Everest, I think it's something I'd sure like to try!"

"Great!"

Martyn looked at his watch and frowned. "Hey, it'll be getting dark soon. We'd better consider if and when we're going to be heading back to your place."

Reluctantly, Ryan pushed himself away from the photos on the table, while Martyn rinsed out the cups. Then they headed down to the dock.

In the shelter of the dock, the water was calm, and a light breeze ruffled Ryan's hair. But farther out in the inlet, the small whitecaps still danced. For a minute Martyn studied the inlet, and then he turned to Ryan.

"Well, Ry, it looks pretty much the way it did before we left your place." He looked at his nephew. "I think we'll be okay, but it's your call."

Ryan crouched down and, for a few moments, silently looked out at the whitecaps. Then he stood up and picked up his life jacket. "I think that it'll be okay." He took a deep breath and grinned at his uncle. "Let's give it our best shot!"

They put on their life jackets, stepped into the canoe, and started paddling back across the inlet to Ryan's home.

Again, as they reached the middle of the channel, the chop grew heavy, the canoe was tossed about, and waves crashed over the bow into Ryan's lap. This time, though, Ryan held on to his paddle, working his way through the rough water until they cleared it. Then they paddled smoothly over to Ryan's dock.

As he got out of the canoe, Ryan turned to his uncle, his eyes shining. "Uncle Martyn, before we left your dock, I visualized myself paddling hard through the waves. I think it worked!"

Martyn smiled in response. "Great, Ryan! Now just think of

visualization as building a mental muscle–the more you use it, the stronger it gets."

"Are you coming up to the house?"

"Not today. I want to get back before I lose the light. But tell your folks that I'll drop by tomorrow on my way into town." Martyn patted Ryan's shoulder. "By the way, have you given any more thought to skipping school tomorrow?"

Ryan looked out at the water, and then turned back to his uncle. "I'll probably go." He grinned. "Yeah, I'm going–I've got a little Everest I want to tackle."

* * * * * * *

The next afternoon, Ryan was on his dock waiting as his uncle's canoe approached.

"Well?" Martyn asked, as he climbed out of the boat and began to tie it up. "How did it go?"

Ryan grinned broadly. "You're looking at the new goalkeeper on the tournament team!"

"That's great, Ry! I knew you could do it!"

Ryan let out a long breath. "You know, last night, I couldn't sleep." He smiled shyly at his uncle. "I tried to think about everything you said, about the visualization and stuff." He looked out over the water. "But I was still scared. I just wasn't sure that I could try out and fail in front of all those other guys. I could see myself missing easy shots, fumbling the ball, doing everything wrong, and all of them were laughing at me–it was awful!"

Ryan turned to his uncle and grinned. "So I decided to try out and *succeed!* I imagined myself going through the moves smooth and fast, perfect block, save after save." He laughed. "After a while,

I could really see it happening."

Ryan's face grew serious. "Of course, when I woke up this morning, I started to feel nervous all over again. I couldn't even eat breakfast because my stomach was all in knots." He looked out over the inlet. "So, I came down here before I went to school. And I thought about yesterday, and about the difference between paddling over and paddling back." Ryan looked at his uncle. "I thought about you, and Everest. And I decided that I had to try. So I did."

Ryan's eyes lit up. "It was so cool! It was just like last night, when I visualized it! Only today it was real. I played the best that I've ever played, and it felt totally right. It felt great! I set out to do it, and I did it!" Ryan turned to his uncle. "You know what I mean?" Then he laughed. "What am I saying–of course you do. You've climbed Everest!"

Martyn hugged his nephew and smiled. "And now, in your own way, so have you."

Dan Culver was a remarkable man, and one not easily forgotten. In 1990 he became the fifth Canadian to conquer Mount Everest, and in 1993, he and partner Jim Haberl became the first Canadians to summit K2, earning them the Governor General's Meritorious Service Award. Sadly, Dan died on his descent from K2, but his legacy and spirit live on. Most of his estate was used to help purchase Jedediah Island on the west coast of British Columbia, now a unique and popular Marine Park. The Dan Culver Follow Your Dream Foundation continues in Dan's footsteps in protecting the environment and promoting youth leadership.

The Dan Culver Follow Your Dream Foundation www.island.net/dcdreams/